Disney · PIXAR
THE GOOD DINOSAUR

PaRRagon

Bath · New York · Cologne · Melbourne · Delhi
Hong Kong · Shenzhen · Singapore · Amsterdam

A long time ago, there lived two
dinosaurs called Henry and Ida.
They lived on a farm with their
three children – Buck, Libby
and Arlo.

Arlo was the youngest and afraid
of everything! Most of all, Arlo was
afraid of the wilderness beyond the
family's farm.

One night, Henry took Arlo into the field. Suddenly, an insect landed on Arlo's nose. Arlo was scared, but Poppa blew gently on the insect – and it glowed!

Then Poppa swept his tail through the grass, and hundreds of fireflies flew into the sky. Arlo was amazed.

The next day, Poppa discovered a critter eating their food.
"You're gonna catch that critter!" he told Arlo.
Arlo was afraid, but he wanted to make his Poppa proud.
As Arlo guarded the silo, he heard something get caught in
Poppa's trap. That's when he got his first look at the critter –
it was a human boy! Arlo didn't want to harm him, so he let him go.

Henry wasn't pleased when he saw the empty trap. He decided to teach his son a lesson by taking him into the wilderness to find the critter. But while they were gone, a terrifying storm caused the river to overflow and poor Poppa was swept away in a flood! Horrified, Arlo watched his Poppa disappear.

With Poppa gone, the family had to work very hard to keep the farm going. Arlo was determined to help take care of his family.

One day, Arlo caught the critter stealing corn again. As he and the critter fought, they tumbled backwards into the river.

"Momma!" Arlo cried, but he had been swept too far away for anyone to hear. The river carried Arlo away. Then – BAM! The little dinosaur hit his head on a rock and he was pulled under by the current.

When Arlo awoke, he had no idea where he was.
He was alone and the wilderness was all around him.
Suddenly, Arlo heard a howl. Standing on the
clifftop above him was the critter.

"You!" shouted Arlo angrily. "This is all your fault!" Furious, he tried to climb up the cliff to get at the little boy. But the critter wasn't afraid.

The critter scampered off, leaving the dinosaur all alone.
Arlo was scared, hungry and tired.

Before long it started to get dark, and Arlo felt raindrops
on his head.

Arlo decided to build a shelter using twigs and branches.
Once his shelter was complete, he curled up beneath its
leaky roof and tried to sleep. But then he heard something
rustling in the bushes outside, heading in his direction....

It was ... the boy! He had brought Arlo
a branch of berries, and that's when the
dinosaur and the boy became friends.
Arlo gave the boy a name – Spot.

Spot couldn't talk, but he and Arlo found
a way of communicating.

Arlo learned that Spot had lost his family,
just as the dinosaur had lost his Poppa.

A few days later, Arlo and Spot met a family of T. rexes called Butch, Ramsey and Nash. They had lost their herd of longhorns.

Arlo offered to help the T. rexes if they could show him the way home. Butch agreed, and Spot tracked down the longhorns. But a nasty surprise lay in wait....

Raptors! This gang of feathery crooks had stolen the longhorns, and weren't going to give them up without a fight. Brave Arlo helped his new friends.

"You're one tough kid," Butch told Arlo.

As promised, the T. rexes helped Arlo and Spot find the direction home, and the pair continued on their journey.

Spot climbed atop Arlo's head and pointed towards the sky. Above the clouds was the most beautiful sunset they had ever seen.

As Arlo and Spot made their way along the mountain pass,
a storm was brewing.

Suddenly, a pack of Pterodactyls swooped down and caught
hold of Spot and whisked him up and away!

Arlo gave chase and found Spot down by the river. Arlo felt
a surge of courage in his heart and charged at the Pterodactyls,
driving them away.

The storm was raging now, and suddenly the river burst its banks!
Arlo and Spot were swept away in the flood. The dinosaur could
see his friend, but he couldn't reach him. Arlo reached Spot just as
they tumbled over a waterfall. The two friends clung to each other
as they fell into the river far, far below.

Arlo climbed ashore holding his friend. They were okay.

Arlo and Spot set off once again. Suddenly, they heard a howl and a human family appeared.

Arlo knew what he had to do. Even though he didn't want to lose Spot, he let him go. The two friends cried as they said goodbye.

Arlo carried on alone and, before long, he saw
something that made him very happy – the farm!
At last, Arlo was home.